I0743077

Fee Fie Foh Fum

Barb Howard

Fee Fie Foh Fum

Radical Bookshop and Press
4838 Richard Road SW, Suite 300
Calgary, AB T3E 6L1

Copyright 2021 by Radical Bookshop and Press

FIC029000 - Fiction, Short Stories

All rights reserved. No part of this publication may be reproduced, stored in a retrieval system or transmited in any form or by any means, electronic, mechanical, photocopying, recording or otherwise without the prior permision of the author.

Chinook Blast Collection
Volume 1
February 1, 2021

Editors: Lexie Angelo
Cover Design: Lexie Angelo

ISBN-13: 978-1-990201-08-0

Printed in the United States

Typeset in Capitolina

*To Marilyn Ledingham and decades
of full moon adventures*

contents

Fee Fie Foh Fum

"Hello old friend," the woman says as she pushes her grocery cart towards me. She looks familiar, about my size, wearing jeans, a puffy jacket, Sorel boots and a toque — like most of the women in this town, me included. But I can't place her. "I'm Bonnie, from high school," she says when she reaches me.

Cripes, high school. That was a couple of decades ago. In the city. Something about Bonnie makes me think maybe I know her from the volleyball team. Too short for a hitter or a middle. Kat and I were setters. Maybe this woman was on the junior squad?

"Hey," I say. "How are you doing?"

"I'm renting a place out here," Bonnie says. "Moved in yesterday."

I offer a few small-town tips, like when the post office is the least busy, what day the grocery store gets fresh produce, and what time the snowplows usually come through to clear the road. I'm not great at conversation and Bonnie doesn't fill the spaces with comfortable chatter either, like Kat does. But Bonnie sticks with me while I do my shopping. Occasionally she puts the same item in her cart as I put in mine. Same brand of chia granola bars. Same number of Gala apples. We check out side-by-side — both cashier stations are open today.

"Let's get together for a cross-country ski," Bonnie says, as we navigate our carts through the snowy parking lot.

"For sure," I say. I wonder how she knows that I ski and then laugh at the thought — everyone around here skis. I stop at my car and give her a friendly goodbye wave. She waves back but keeps looking at me as she pushes her cart. Maybe she's looking at my car. I survey my car — nothing out of the ordinary, no flat tire or dented side. Just a car.

I open the hatch and load in my groceries. When I walk around to the driver's seat, I notice my friend Kat in the car next to mine. She points in Bonnie's direction and then pulls her toque down over her eyes. I rap on her window. She lowers it. I reach in and pull up on her giant pompom — it's almost the size of her head — to lift her toque off her face.

"Ack! Bonnie Quacker from high school," Kat squeals. "What's she doing out here?"

"Moved here yesterday," I say. "She caught me off guard in the cereal aisle."

"I knew it was her right away," Kat says. "That walk. Toes pointed out like a duck. Bonnie the ball girl. I saw her go into the grocery store right after you. I thought I'd wait in my car to get your report."

"Not much to report. I barely remember her. She wants to go for a ski."

"She probably isn't any good," Kat says.

"She looks fit," I say.

"Oh, come on. It's Bonnie Quacker."

Kat gets out of her car as I get into mine.

"See you at yoga tonight," she calls. She does an exaggerated duck walk through the snow to the grocery store.

On my drive home, I recall more memories about Bonnie, prompted by Kat saying she was the ball girl. Bonnie had a pudgy face in high school. And short hair, back when the rest of us had long feathered hair. And, yes, a duck walk that was worse when she ran around the gym to retrieve the volleyballs from our drills. Like Charlie Chaplin on amphetamines. One time when I was late getting out of the locker room after a game, the only player left, Bonnie came thumping down the stairs saying, "Fee Fie Foh Fum." To be funny, I guess. But I felt an odd little worry in the pit of my stomach, and I snuck out of the locker room when she was 'Fee Fie Foh Fum'-ing through the shower stalls. I'm not sure why I was worried. She probably didn't even know I was in there.

Later that night when I arrive at the community centre for drop-in yoga, there are already several pairs of Sorels in the lobby. I step out of my boots and pad into the gym. It's a huge room and so cold that we do yoga with our toques on. Several people sit cross-legged on their mats, waiting for class to begin. I see Kat's giant pompom near the front. That's noteworthy because she usually arrives late for everything. I see the back of a woman whose toque-top I don't recognize — hers has a Nordic-style tassel. When I walk by, I realize it's Bonnie. I hadn't noticed the tassel in the grocery store.

"Hello you," Bonnie says as I walk by. "Saved you a spot." She points to the floor beside her.

"Thanks," I say. I'm not sure why she felt the need to save me a spot. There is no shortage of space in the gym. There's never more than ten people in the class and there's an entire gym's worth of space. I unroll my mat beside her, at a slightly further distance than she has indicated. I sit cross-legged on it, close my eyes. I sense Bonnie might be looking at me. So, I glance back at her. She smiles at me — a closed-lip smile — then leans towards me and grabs the edge of my mat with both hands. She slides my mat, with me on it, a few inches closer to her.

Before I can get over my surprise, the teacher starts talking at the front of the room. I follow her cues, lie on my back, knees to chest. Rock. Sit up. Slowly sway my head from side to side. I try not to think about Bonnie doing the same motions beside me.

The teacher leads us through more poses. For this crowd, yoga is more of a stretch class than true yoga. Yoga for Sports, it's called — which means we're all here with tight hamstrings, rather than deep thoughts. At the end of the class, Bonnie turns to me and gives me a long solemn namaste, bows her head all the way to the floor. I figure she must have gone to a serious yoga place in the city.

While Bonnie's forehead is still touching the floor, Kat wanders over to my mat. She's walking with her toes out. I don't know how she can be so sure that Bonnie won't notice. Or maybe Bonnie does notice, because after she brings her head up from her bow she stands, rolls her mat super tight, wraps one hand in a chokehold around its middle, and walks out of the gym. With Bonnie out of ear shot, Kat leans over.

"How'd Bonnie know you were coming to yoga tonight?" Kat asks.

"Maybe she heard you in the parking lot today," I suggest.

"She had a crush on you. She probably still does."

"I have no recollection of that," I mutter as I roll up my mat.

"You never seem to recollect anything from high school."

"It was just high school."

"Some people have more complicated memories," Kat says. Then she winces. "I hope she doesn't come into my clinic to get that walk fixed."

As we're walking out of the gym I ask, "Is her last name really Quacker?"

"Of course not," Kat says. "The coach gave her that name. And then there was that rumour that Bonnie broke into the Phys Ed office and slashed up the coach's team jacket."

Bonnie is still in the lobby when we arrive. She has her Sorels on and is busy doing up the laces. Most of us keep ours in a permanent knot. Bonnie's boots are brand new, not broken down at the heels or with worn felt at the top like all the other boots at the door.

She looks up from her lace-tying and says to me, "For a minute, when I saw you at the grocery store today, I thought maybe you didn't recognize me."

"Sure I did," I say. "You were with the volleyball team."

"Team assistant," she says. She pulls off her Nordic toque and a sweep of long hair falls onto her shoulders. She shakes it, lets it drape on her shoulders like a blonde blanket. It's an unusual sight. Most women here, like Kat and me, have short hair.

"Hi Bonnie," Kat says.

"Oh, hi Kat," Bonnie says, turning to acknowledge Kat briefly. Bonnie pulls her toque back on, tucks her hair into it, and dons her puffy jacket.

"What brings you to town?" Kat asks.

"I was living in the city, working for a security firm. But after my husband died, I thought I'd retire early and try the small-town life."

"I'm sorry about your husband," Kat says.

Bonnie, zipping her jacket, says, "It was expected."

Kat raises an eyebrow at me and twirls her finger around her ear in a cuckoo gesture.

Bonnie tucks her yoga mat under her arm and pushes open the door. A blast of cold air laced with light snow enters the lobby but before she exits, she says, "I hear you're the town physio."

"That's right," Kat confirms.

"Congratulations," Bonnie says, and lets the door clang shut behind her.

"Did she try out for the volleyball team?" I ask Kat.

"You do live in your own world. She got cut. You and I were the setters. You played. I warmed the bench."

"You played too," I argue.

"No, I did not," Kat says.

"Oh well," I say. "Why are we talking about high school? Who cares?"

A few days later, Kat and I are out for our weekly cross-country ski. She arrives late but only by a few minutes this time. She arrives late so often that we have a rule that if twenty minutes pass and she's not there, I start skiing without her. We've been classic skiing together for years. It's handy. Neither of us have got into skate skiing yet. Maybe next year. I'm in front. *Kick and glide, kick and glide, kick and glide.* I'm having trouble getting into my rhythm because I'm thinking about Bonnie. I wonder if I should have invited her to join us on this ski when I saw her at yoga? But why change up an activity that has been working for me and Kat all these years? Bonnie will find someone else to ski with. *Kick and glide, kick and glide.* I check over my shoulder. It looks like Kat is having trouble with her wax and her kick is slipping. I stop in a spot where the sun is breaking through the trees and wait for her to catch up.

When Kat reaches me, she takes off her skis, pulls a blue wax cylinder and a square cork out of her pocket.

"I'll try some of this," she says. After she crayons the wax on the centre of the underside of her skis, she looks at me asks, "Don't you think it's creepy that Bonnie has come to town?"

"No. When you arrived here a couple of years after me, I didn't think it was creepy."

"Because we're friends," Kat says. She rubs the wax into her skis with the cork, looks at me again. "Haven't you noticed that wherever you are, Bonnie shows up?"

"It's a small town," I say. "We're bound to be in the same places."

"She's a nut," Kat says, stuffing the cork and wax back into her pocket.

Kat steps into her skis and gives me her standard carry-on signal — a two-arm swing, like an underhand toss of ball, towards the trail. There's a steep climb coming up and I want to gather speed before I have to herringbone, so I stride ahead. Kat won't be too far behind. She's used to me shooting out front.

When we're back at our cars at the trailhead parking lot, Kat mentions the full moon on the weekend. "Do you want to ski or go to yoga? Same night."

"Both," I say. "We have to wait until the moon is up anyway. May as well go to yoga first."

Kat agrees. She's always game. But she reminds me that the forecast is for bitter cold.

I'm not worried about the weather. We've done lots of full moon skis. And lots of cold ones. The attraction is skiing at night in the moonlight. It doesn't always pan out. Often, it's cloudy and we have to use headlamps — so technically it could be any night. But still, it's a ski.

During the week, Kat's suspicion proves correct. Bonnie *is* everywhere. At the post office when I pick up my mail, she's there reading the numbers on all the boxes. I wonder if she's looking for her own. She has the same tasselled toque, puffy jacket, and duck stance. I quietly open my mailbox and grab the few envelopes inside. I don't think Bonnie sees me. At least, she doesn't turn around. The next day, when I fill up my car at the gas station, she's there inside the convenience store, buying a 6-pack of energy drinks. She comes out of the store, holding the drinks in one hand, and waving at me with the other. I stop the gas pump as I wave back even though my tank isn't full, and I get in my car to drive away. I don't check the rear-view mirror. The feeling in my gut forces me to keep moving.

At the local coffee shop, The Hill of Beans, I plan to do some work on my laptop, drink a coffee and eat a bagel sandwich. I'm a gas marketer so I can work anywhere with Wi-Fi. But when I'm at the counter about to place my order, I see Bonnie coming through the door. I change plans and take my sandwich and coffee to go. I exit through the side door, tucking my mitts under my arm.

Once I'm in my car, I set my coffee in the cupholder, my sandwich on the dash, and my laptop on the passenger seat. But I discover I only have one mitt. Must have dropped the other. I crack open the door and scan the pavement to see if I dropped it beside the car. The door suddenly swings wider, and I have to brace myself by putting my foot on the ground to keep from tipping out of the vehicle.

"Missing your mitt?" Bonnie asks. Her hand is on the trim of the car door. Her fingers reach around and onto the inside of the window glass.

"I am," I say, as I try to discreetly tug the car door towards me. But Bonnie has a solid grip. She steps around the door.

"Here," she says, setting my mitt on the thigh of my leg that is outside of the car. She pats my thigh a few times then steps back.

"Thanks." I toss the mitt on the passenger seat. There's a moment of silence and then I tug on the door again. Bonnie holds it.

"Gotta go," I say. "Expecting a call from work."

I bring my leg into the car. Put both my hands on the door handle and pull as hard as I can. The door slams shut. My sandwich flips from the dash to the floor. I rush to press the door lock button, accidentally press a window button that lowers the rear passenger-side window. Leaving the window down, I start the car, fumble the gear shift into reverse and back my car out of the lot. Once I am on the main road, I glance at the sandwich innards spilled all over the floormat and laugh at myself, at the ridiculous adrenaline rush I'm still feeling. What was I scared of? It's not like Bonnie was going to crawl into the car on top of me. I take a few deep breaths. I press the button to close the rear window. Then reach for my coffee, take a sip even though my hand is shaking a bit.

By the time yoga night rolls around I fully expect Bonnie to be there. So, I'm surprised when I don't see her tasselled toque when I enter the gym. I unroll my mat. The instructor quiets the room and the class starts. Kat comes into the gym, late, and sets up beside me. We do cat and cow poses.

"Where's your sidekick?" Kat whispers.

I shrug as though Bonnie is no big deal. But without her around I do feel relief as the yoga class starts. I flow through the poses. The instructor has us all turn to face the side wall to do some squats. And then we turn to the back of the room for standing tree poses.

That's when I see Bonnie.

She's sitting against the back wall in her Nordic toque and street clothes. Arms crossed. Glaring. I turn to face the front of the room, get into a kneeling position and settle into a child's pose with my eyes fixed at the mat rather than at Bonnie, for the rest of the class.

When the class is over, Bonnie is no longer at the back of the room.

"Did you see the Quacker?" Kat asks, as we walk out of the gym together. "That was not a peaceful yoga expression on her face."

"I saw her," I say. "Maybe she's hurt or something."

"Probably 'or something,'" Kat says.

Bonnie is standing in the lobby. She watches as Kat and I pull wind pants over our yoga tights and layer-up with our puffy jackets, wind breakers and neck tubes.

"Are you guys really going skiing?" Bonnie asks.

"We have a full moon tradition," Kat says.

Bonnie looks directly at me. "I thought you and I were going to go for a ski."

"We'll do that sometime," I assure her. I pull on my ski gloves and top them with my overmitts. I point to Kat with my mittened hand and say, "See you at the trailhead."

When I get to the trailhead parking lot, I slide my seat away from the steering wheel and use the extra room to change out of my Sorels and into my ski boots. I try not to overheat in the vehicle, which warmed up on the drive. I wonder where the heck Kat is. Maybe she's having car trouble, after all it's -30ºC. I check my phone for messages even though cell service in this lot is terrible. Nothing. I try to send Kat a text. *Where r u?* It fails.

I wait for almost half an hour, ten minutes longer than I usually would – mainly because it's cold and a night ski. Maybe someone from the yoga class stopped Kat with a physio question. That's happened before. But it's inconsiderate of her to let me sit here in the dark — no moon showing yet — and cold. I have to either start skiing to warm up or take off some layers and turn the car on. Getting too hot in the car will result in sweat and then a dangerous chill when I finally get skiing.

I step out of the car. Do a few jumping jacks and leg swings to stay warm. I stand impatiently for a moment, feeling the cold starting to seep through my layers of clothing. Time's up, I decide. I've waited long enough. I turn on my headlamp, snap into my skis, slip my pole straps over my mitts, and start skiing. If I slow my stride, Kat will catch up. She always does.

Kat and I ski the same route on our full moon skis: a gradual curving climb up to the open ridge, and then a steep switchback route back down through the trees to the parking lot. I set off at a slow steady pace. *Kick and glide.* The cold snow squeaks under the pressure of my pole plants. Although this might be her record for lateness, Kat will show up. Halfway up the climb, I look down to the trailhead and, sure enough, see headlights pulling into the parking lot. Since my headlamp is on, Kat will be able to see where I'm at on the trail. I slow my skiing even more to a point where I can stay almost warm but give Kat a chance to catch up more quickly. The car lights go out, a headlamp turns on, she must be starting the route.

My body starts to chill. I open and close my hands to keep the circulation flowing to my fingers. Every once in a while, I check over my shoulder to make sure the headlamp is closing the gap. Up in the sky, the soft cloud cover slides away so the moon, combined with the reflection off the snow, now supplies enough light to see clearly. I click my headlamp off but Kat keeps hers on. Maybe she is working so hard that she doesn't realize she doesn't need it anymore. I keep moving towards the ridge — but in an exaggerated manner with big arm swings and wide strides — that keeps my pace slow but also keeps the blood flowing to my extremities.

When I reach the top of the ridge, I turn to see if Kat is close. At the summit, there is a massive boulder, a smooth glacial erratic. Sometimes we lean our bums against it while we admire the moon and sometimes we share a snack or a drink. But it's too cold tonight. I stop a few meters past the boulder. I keep my skis in the track, sliding them back and forth to keep warm. I'll go as soon as Kat reaches me.

Kat skis around the final curve to the summit, her headlight is not aimed directly at me and so I get my first side view of her silhouette. She wears her big pompom toque. It's impractical for cross-country skiing but she always wears it anyway. But her stride is different tonight. Her stance is more upright, arms wider apart than usual. She approaches the big erratic. During the moments when she is behind the rock, I can't see her, but I can hear the push of her skis and poles, and that feeling in my gut comes back. When she skis into view again, I see a closer version of her profile. And notice a long tress of hair poking out of the toque. Bonnie.

I spend no time wondering how Bonnie is in Kat's clothing. In Kat's toque. She would never give up that toque. I kick up my skis and drive my poles into the snow, gathering momentum as fast as possible. A shoulder check reveals that Bonnie has picked up her speed, too. The light from her headlamp draws nearer and brighter. At the edge of the clearing, I start what I already know will be a recklessly fast descent through the trees — an attempt to get to my car before Bonnie catches me. She yells. Initially, the distance between us is great enough that I can't distinguish the words. But as I skid around a sharp turn I clearly hear, "Fee fie foh fum!"

ABOUT THE AUTHOR

Barb Howard is a former Author in Residence for the Calgary Public Library. Her short story collection Western Taxidermy (NeWest Press) won the Canadian Authors' Association Exporting Alberta Award and was a finalist at the international High Plains Book Awards. Her work has been shortlisted several times for Alberta Literary Awards and she won the 2009 Howard O'Hagan Award for Short Story.

Barb's novel Happy Sands is forthcoming from University of Calgary Press. Her previous novels include Notes For Monday (Recliner Books), Whipstock (NeWest Press) and The Dewpoint Show (Fitzhenry & Whiteside). She is co-editor of the nonfiction anthology Embedded on the Home Front: Where Military and Civilian Lives Converge (Heritage House).

Barb has a BA in Canadian Literature from UBC, a law degree from Dalhousie and an MA in Creative Writing from the University of Calgary.

www.barbhoward.ca

SPECIAL THANKS

Chinook Blast Festival

The City of Calgary

Tourism Calgary

Calgary Municipal Land Corporation

Calgary Arts Development

Calgary Public Library

IngramSpark

www.ingramcontent.com/pod-product-compliance
Lightning Source LLC
Chambersburg PA
CBHW071352200726
48293CB00008B/2623